T0197375

To order additional copies of this book, contact:
Xlibris
1-888-795-4274
www.Xlibris.com
Orders@Xlibris.com

Hair like Mine

Emma Sparkes

Dedication

For My Mother, who has always helped me make sense of my dreams,
My Father, who pointed out the perfect verse to go along with this story,
And for the incredible family God has given me to
help and support me through everything.

"I praise You, for I am fearfully and wonderfully made."
Psalms 139:14

On top of my head I had funny hair.
Funny hair that went everywhere.
Butterflies and flowers were weaved into my curls.
With stems and leaves and branches braided in the swirls and twirls.

I loved my funny hair and could stare for hours in the mirror,
At all the butterflies fluttering far away then nearer.
I couldn't wait to show the world, they'd want to see for sure,
This incredible, wonderful hair of mine, they had never seen before.

But this silly world, that embraced me just before,
Rejected and then ridiculed this hair that I adored.
Was the world right? Was this hair of mine a mess?
Should I be embarrassed of my hair unlike the rest?

So I shooed away the butterflies and cut the shameful flowers.
I plucked the leaves and branches and jumped into the shower.
I scrubbed and soaped and rinsed, then dried off with a towel,
But when I looked into the mirror what I saw was oh so foul!

The scrubs and dubs and plucks and shoos hadn't worked on me.
All that funny hair came back and had multiplied by three.
What was I supposed to do with this head of bugs and strays?
The only option that I had was to run so far away.

4

I flew past the park as fast as I could. There were people everywhere.
I didn't want to stop and see the way they would pause and stare.
I passed the cute cafe and the baker with his rolls.
Past all the little shops in town where so often I had strolled.

I ran so hard I didn't notice at all,
The town that I was fleeing was getting rather small.
I would have kept on running, but seemingly out of nowhere,
A tiny pile of painted rocks tripped and flung me through the air.

I looked to see just what it was that had stopped my great escape.
This funny rock began to glow and I began to shake.
I didn't know what to do with this simple yet strange pebble,
So I picked it up then put it down and felt it start to tremble.

This is where things got crazy, the rocks began to dance.
They swayed and spun and moved around, and with them I did prance.
They continued to spin and shift and with a softish patter,
It came up from beneath the rocks, and what came up was a ladder.

This Ladder rose up past the trees.
It's as if the clouds were calling me.
My curiosity was going wild I had to know for sure.
Where did this odd ladder go, just to the clouds or more?

I climbed and climbed and with my legs getting shaky,
I reached up, touched a cloud and took in a site worth taking.
I stepped off the ladder and it's hard to describe.
The most incredible, wonderful feeling I began to feel inside.

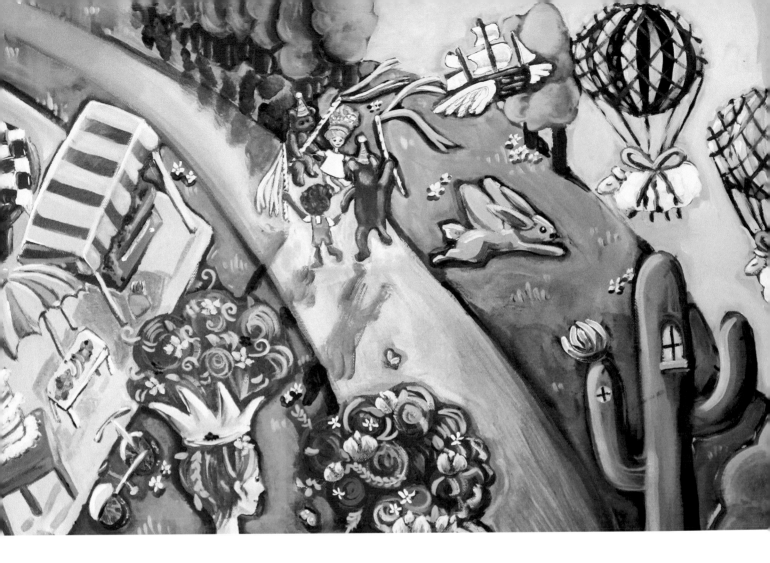

I had climbed above the clouds and what I found was amazing,
The most colorful world I'd ever seen and everything here was crazy.
This bright new world was full of odd things,
Like dancing bears and rabbits with wings.

I stopped to watch people dancing about.
Was there more to this place? I had to find out.
I was so distracted taking in the scene.
I hadn't even noticed the girl behind me.

S he tapped me on the shoulder and when I turned around,
She had crazy hair like me and on top she wore a crown.
"Hello there, how was the climb?
You got here fast, we'll have plenty of time."

Plenty of time for what I wondered?
But before I could ask, my words were blundered.
I couldn't believe what came down from the sky,
A giant flying turtle, here to take us for a ride.

11

We flew on his polished green shell, and the girl, she showed me around.
The houses were made of mushrooms, and sat just outside of town.
There were some people just like me, with mounds of crazy hair.
They would wave and smile at me and I was happy to be there.

The turtle dropped us off, I waved as he flew away.
I turned to the girl with hair like mine to hear what she had to say.
The problem is I can't recall what it was she said at all.
But what was this world and why was I here? How did she know I was coming?
Hadn't it been just by chance that I hit those rocks while running?

Those people we flew by, with crazy hair like mine,
Didn't care if people stared and adored their hair like I.
I backed my way down the ladder to tell the world below,
All about my crazy day starting with a stone that I saw glow.

Back on the ground and headed towards town,
I watched as the ladder began to come down.
The rocks lost their glow and somehow I know,
I won't get to go back I belong here below.

That's when I woke up. You see,
To my dismay it was all a dream.

And I tell you this mother,
Because now I wonder.

"What does it mean, this dream that I dreamed?"
"Well my sweet girl, it's about deciding instead,
To love yourself inside and out, no matter what is on top of your head."